Where Is Home, Little Pip?

A brilliant editor once asked me if I could write a story
about a lost penguin. I dedicate this book to
that editor and friend, Emma Dryden. A penguin saga
was hatched from one small request.
—K. W.

For Florence and Verity
—J. C.

Margaret K. McElderry Books • An imprint of Simon & Schuster Children's Publishing Division
• 1230 Avenue of the Americas, New York, New York 10020 • Text copyright © 2008 by Karma
Wilson • Illustrations copyright © 2008 by Jane Chapman • All rights reserved, including the
right of reproduction in whole or in part in any form. • Book design by Sonia Chaghatzbanian
The text for this book is set in Lucida Bright. • The illustrations for this book are rendered in
acrylic. • Manufactured in China • 10 9 8 7 6 5 4 3 2 1 • Library of Congress Cataloging-in-
Publication Data • Wilson, Karma. • Where is home, Little Pip? / Karma Wilson ; illustrated by
Jane Chapman. —1st ed. • p. cm. • Summary: After Little Pip the penguin gets lost, she meets a
whale, a Kelp Gull, and sled dogs who cannot help her, but with the aid of her family's song, home
finds her. • ISBN-13: 978-0-689-85983-0 • ISBN-10: 0-689-85983-X • [1. Penguins—Fiction.
2. Animals—Infancy—Fiction. 3. Animals—Fiction. 4. Lost children—Fiction. 5. Antarctica—
Fiction.] • I. Chapman, Jane, 1970- ill. II. Title. • PZ7.W69656Wh 2008 • [E]—dc22 • 2006019094

FIRST
EDITION

Where Is Home, Little Pip?

Karma Wilson   illustrated by **Jane Chapman**

Margaret K. McElderry Books
New York London Toronto Sydney

Pip was hatched in a nest made of pebbles on the cold Antarctic shore. She was as fluffy as new-fallen snow—and small even for a baby penguin.

Every day Pip played.

Whooosh . . . Whiiiish . . . "WHEEEEEE!!!!!"

Mama and Papa always said, "Don't wander far, Little Pip." And she didn't.

Every night Pip's parents sang:

"Our home is where the land is free
from hill or mountain, twig or tree,
in our pebbly nest by the stormy sea,
where Mama and Papa and Pip
makes three."

Pip grew. She needed more and more food. Mama and Papa constantly fished to keep up with Pip's belly. They never left her for long and always warned, "Don't wander far, Little Pip." And she didn't.

Until . . .

. . . one day Pip saw a feather.

It glittered black against the white ice.

Pip chased after it.

FLAP, FLAP, SLAP

But when she got close,
—*POOF!*—a gust of freezing wind fluttered the feather away.

FLAP, FLAP, SLAP

Pip chased.

And chased.

And chased.

"Got you!" she cried.

But when she turned for home . . .
home wasn't there.

As far as Pip could see, there was no pebbly nest . . .
no penguins . . .
and worst of all, no Mama and Papa!

"Where is home?" Pip cried. Nobody answered.
So Pip set off to look.

Soon she heard

SWISH! SWISH!

There was a huge plume in the sea. A mighty blue whale poked her gigantic head from the water.

Pip waddled close and said, "Hello! Can you tell me, where is home?"

The whale smiled. "Yes, little one, I can."

SPLASH!

She slapped her mighty tail and said,

"Home is under the oceans deep,
by the coral beds where the minnows sleep,
where fish are in schools and sea creatures creep,
where my babies and I swim and leap."

Pip frowned. "But that's not *my* home," she said.
"I'm sorry," said the whale. "But that's the home I know."
"Thank you, anyway," said Pip. She plodded on.

After a bit, Pip saw
a Kelp Gull pecking a shell.

"Hello!" said Pip.
"Can you tell me,
where is home?"

"*Squawk!*

Yes, little penguin," said the bird. "I think
I can." She ruffled her feathers and said,

"*On the craggy cliffs, in a humble nest,*
with sea to the east and land to the west,
in a cozy crevice where shelter is best,
home is where my little chicks rest."

Pip frowned. "But that's not *my* home," she said.
The bird shook her head sadly. "*Squawk!*
Dreadful, I'm sure. But that's the home I know."

"Oh, well," said Pip.
"I'll keep looking."

Pip slumped along. She had walked far when she saw something strange indeed—a tall, two-legged creature being pulled by many four-legged creatures.

When the creatures were close,
Pip called, "Hello, strangers! Can
you tell me, where is home?"

The tall creature said something, but Pip
couldn't make out the words. One of the
four-legged creatures said, "*Woof!*
Don't mind him. I can answer that, little
bird!" She wagged her tail and said,

"Across the ocean far away,
after sailing a ship for many a day,
on the sandy shore there's a house weathered gray—
home is where my puppies play!"

Pip frowned. "But that's not *my* home," she said.

"*Woof!*" said the creature. "What a shame. That's the home I know."

"Nice meeting you," said Pip. "I must keep searching."

And she did.

But the more Pip looked,

the more lost she became.

Finally, Pip stopped. Tears dripped down her cheek and froze solid. Her legs were sore. Her beak was cold. Her eyes were sleepy.

"I want Mama and Papa!" she wailed. "I want home."

Pip couldn't think of anything else to do, so she
thought of Mama and Papa and started to sing:

"Our home is where the land is free
from hill or mountain, twig or tree,
in our pebbly nest by the stormy sea,
where Mama and Papa and Pip makes three."

Suddenly she heard something.

"Pip? Little Pi–i–iiip? Is that you?"

Suddenly she saw something!

"Mama! Papa! Here I am!" cried Pip.

They rushed to meet her.

They hugged.

They kissed.

Mama and Papa danced and
waddled around her.

"Oh, Little Pip!" said Mama.

"We've looked for you all day," said Papa.

"We finally heard you singing!"

As they snuggled, Mama sighed. "After such a long, scary day, you must be exhausted, my dear. Let's sleep."

"Yes, let's," said Papa.

"But aren't we going *home*?" asked Pip.

Mama and Papa kissed Pip on her head.

They asked, "Where is home, Little Pip?" Then they sang this song:

"Where is home? Is it far or near?
Is a pebbly nest what we all hold dear?
No, home is where there's nothing to fear.
Since we're together, home is right here!"

And Little Pip slept, home at last.